For Laurel and John, with love
—K. D.

For Bella, Sofia, Jack, and Finn
—S. C.

atheneum

ATHENEUM BOOKS FOR YOUNG READERS
An imprint of Simon & Schuster Children's Publishing Division
1230 Avenue of the Americas, New York, New York 10020
Text copyright © 2015 by Kelly DiPucchio
Illustrations copyright © 2015 by Scott Campbell
ATHENEUM BOOKS FOR YOUNG READERS is a registered trademark of Simon & Schuster, Inc.
Atheneum logo is a trademark of Simon & Schuster, Inc.
For information about special discounts for bulk purchases, please contact Simon &
Schuster Special Sales at 1-866-506-1949 or business@simonandschuster.com.
The Simon & Schuster Speakers Bureau can bring authors to your live event. For more
information or to book an event, contact the Simon & Schuster Speakers Bureau at
1-866-248-3049 or visit our website at www.simonspeakers.com.
Book design by Sonia Chaghatzbanian
The text for this book is set in Barbera.
The illustrations for this book are rendered in watercolor.
Manufactured in China
1014 SCP
First Edition
2 4 6 8 10 9 7 5 3 1
Library of Congress Cataloging-in-Publication Data
DiPucchio, Kelly S.
Zombie in love 2 + 1 / Kelly DiPucchio ; pictures by Scott Campbell. — 1st ed.
p. cm.
Summary: "Zombie lovebirds Mortimer and Mildred discover a baby on their doorstep.
They're worried sick when the baby sleeps through the night and hardly ever cries. How
will they teach him to be a proper zombie child?"—Provided by publisher.
ISBN 978-1-4424-5937-3 (hardcover)
ISBN 978-1-4424-5938-0 (eBook)
[1. Zombies—Fiction. 2. Babies—Fiction. 3. Humorous stories.] I. Campbell, Scott,
1973– illustrator. II. Title. III. Title: Zombie in love two.
PZ7.D6219Zn 2015
[E]—dc23 2013035913

Zombie in Love 2+1

Kelly DiPucchio

pictures by
Scott Campbell

Atheneum Books for Young Readers

New York London Toronto Sydney New Delhi

Mortimer and Mildred had a problem.

It wasn't a big problem.
It was a *little* problem.

Mortimer and Mildred were thrilled
to be new parents, but they were
also scared to death. Having a baby
wasn't what they expected.

Sonny was a fussy eater.

His teeth were coming in instead
of falling out.

And, worst of all, he was awake *all day* and slept through the night.

Poor Mortimer and Mildred.
They were dead tired. And
worried sick.

They read books and followed
all the advice.

They gave bottles to the baby.

They changed his diaper.

They took him for long walks
in the fresh air.

They even shrieked him lullabies,
but nothing worked.

Mortimer and Mildred racked
their brains and came up with an
idea. They took Sonny to the doctor.

"He sleeps through the night," Mortimer explained.

"And he hardly ever cries," Mildred said nervously.

The doctor looked at the couple strangely.

He checked the baby's bright eyes.

He listened to the baby's
strong heartbeat.

He wiggled the baby's pink toes.

Sonny smiled.

Like this:

"There's nothing wrong with your baby," the doctor said. "I'd say you two are very lucky parents."

Mortimer and Mildred were relieved.

The family went home and filled
their sleepless days reading stories,

and playing peek-a-BOO

and patty-cake.

One evening, many months later, the weary parents awoke feeling a little stiff but rested. Sonny had *finally* slept through the day!

Mortimer and Mildred danced
in the moonlight.

Their celebration was short-lived.

They heard a loud thud. The thud
was followed by an even louder crash.
The frantic parents shuffled to the
nursery.

There on the floor was Sonny.

"Quick!" Mildred shouted. "Grab the camera! Sonny just took his first fall!"

The baby cried.

Like this:

"EEEEEEEEEEEEEEE!

"Do you hear that, dear?" Mortimer asked, beaming with pride. "It's positively terrifying!"

Mortimer picked up his son.

Mildred kissed his boo-boo.

And the three of them smiled.

Like this:

"I'm the luckiest ghoul in the world."
Mildred sighed, gazing into Sonny's
happy face.

"You know what, darling?"
she said to Mortimer. "I think
he has your nose!"

Mortimer tried to blush. "You may be right," he said. "But he definitely gets his brains from you."